A Giant-Sized Day

Written by Deb Eaton

Illustrated by Michele Noiset

Silver Burdett Ginn
A Division of Simon & Schuster
160 Gould Street
Needham Heights, MA 02194-2310

Design and production by Kirchoff/Wohlberg, Inc.

ISBN 0-663-59382-4

4 5 6 7 8 9 10 SP 01 00 99 98 97 96

Once upon a time, a giant named Clad
lived in his giant-sized house.

Clad liked to stay home. Everything there was just his size. He had a giant-sized glass. It was as big as a pail.

4

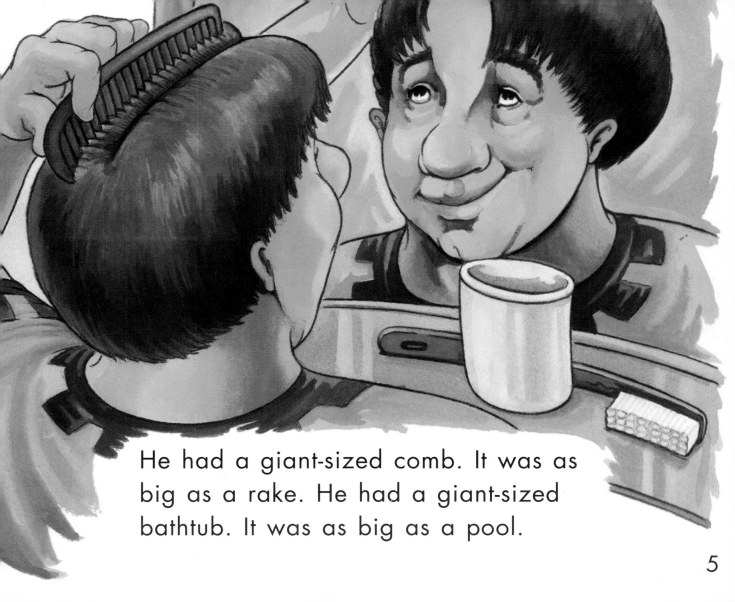

He had a giant-sized comb. It was as big as a rake. He had a giant-sized bathtub. It was as big as a pool.

Every day, Clad ate a giant-sized
breakfast. Then he took a nap.

When he woke up, he played a
giant-sized game. He ate a giant-sized
snack. Then he took a nap.

But one day, Clad was tired of taking naps. And he was tired of staying home. He wanted to try something new.

8

"I think I'll go to the beach," he thought.
"I want to play in the waves."

9

Clad took his hat, and off he went. He tried to take a bus to the beach. But the bus wasn't made for giants.

He tried to take a train to the beach.
But the train wasn't made for giants.

Clad tried to take a sailboat across the lake to the beach.

But the sailboat wasn't made for giants.

Then Clad found a way to get to the
beach. He made giant-sized skates. He
had to put three skates on each foot.

The skates got him all the way to the beach. "Now I can play in the waves," thought Clad.

"But first I'll take a little nap."